Gene Kemp has written many extremely successful children's books, several of which have been Whitbread and Smarties Awards runners-up. Her best-known book, however, is the ever popular and unforgettable winner of the Carnegie Medal and the Other Award, *The Turbulent Term of Tyke Tyler*.

Gene grew up in the Midlands and now lives in Exeter, where she took her degree. She has three children and was once a teacher, but now writes full time, as she has done for many years. As well as children's books, Gene writes for TV and radio.

For Rosi and Jon,
Brendan and Miranda
G.K.

ORCHARD BOOKS
96 Leonard Street, London EC2A 4XD
Orchard Books Australia
32/45-51 Huntley Street, Alexandria, NSW 2015
First published in Great Britain in 2005
A paperback original
ISBN 1 84362 269 6
Text © Gene Kemp 2005
The right of Gene Kemp to be identified as the author of this
work has been asserted by her in accordance with
the Copyright, Designs and Patents Act, 1988.
A CIP catalogue record for this book is
available from the British Library.
3 5 7 9 10 8 6 4
Printed in Great Britain

The Haunted Piccolo

GENE KEMP

ORCHARD BOOKS

Chapter One   Shadow Lane

One sunny September evening, a boy called Luke walked with his grandmother through the dusty, crowded streets of an old city. "Is it much further?" he asked as they wove their way through the busy shoppers, impatient to be finished and get home, away from the cars with horns blaring angrily as their drivers tried also to escape the congested roads. 'I hope this shop doesn't close before we get there,' he added, shouting above a particularly loud hoot just close to his ears.

'We turn off somewhere near, I think,' said his grandmother. 'It's ages since I was here last, but I know the turning is soon. There – there it is. We turn left just past the bank. That's it. We're here.'

As they turned the corner, away from the dust, the heat, the clamour, the cross faces...they entered another world. *Shadow Lane*, said a dusty sign. *No traffic beyond this point.* The noise behind them was swallowed up as they started to walk along the narrow cobbled lane overhung with black and white buildings almost meeting overhead, jutting out over the grimy shops below. Through the dusty windows Luke could just pick out antiques, books, toys, pictures and clothes, rich, strange and old.

Shadow Lane sloped steeply down to two bollards leaning crookedly against each other and, far beyond them, Luke could see the silver gleam of the town's river flowing under a stone bridge that was half overgrown with trees and bushes. The cathedral bells rang out at a quarter to five. The golden sun burned in the sky above the river and the hills beyond as if it would never set, yet Shadow Lane was as dark and sombre as if it had been forgotten.

'Are you sure this is the right place?' asked Luke. He found himself shivering slightly in the shade of the overhung lane. 'It's a bit spooky, Gran.'

The shops appeared to be closed. No one moved, there wasn't even a cat crossing the road or a sparrow sneaking crumbs.

'Yes, yes, this is it. Shadow Lane. I used to come here long ago with your dad when he was little, to buy sheet music. Then I think the place closed, so we went to the big shop in the High Street instead. But someone told me it had reopened and, since it always had the very best instruments, I thought we'd better come back to it.'

Luke had a sudden fleeting memory of his dad coming home smiling, waving some new music book or duet, grabbing Luke and insisting they try out this or that tune together straight away. Never mind tea on the table, or homework to do.

Luke didn't realise he had stopped walking

until Gran put her arm around him comfortingly and moved him on along the lane.

Luke's dad had died a short time ago – a heart attack, completely out of the blue. Luke and his mother were devastated. But the loss seemed to Luke to have changed his mother too, into a tired, easily angered person, cross at everything, and especially impatient with Luke. His gran had come to live with them, so that his mum could work full time to support them. But even with Gran there to help out, it was now a home where no one ever laughed. Luke missed the laughter.

Down, down, down they descended the steep slope of the lane till they were almost at the bottom. Now they could see the river clearly, sliding swiftly past the quay on its way to the sea, shining bright beyond Shadow Lane's dark tunnel.

'Everywhere's shut.' Luke felt uneasy.

'No, no. It's all right, Luke. Look! It's here. I knew where it was all the time,' said Gran.

They stopped where the bumpy pavement rose up above uneven steps that led down to a door with peeling paint and a grimy window full of musical instruments. They gleamed against the darkness inside the shop: trumpets, violins, guitars, saxophones, recorders and an old tin whistle. Round the window hung sheet music, some of it new and shining, some old and brown, curling round the edges. Screwing up his eyes, Luke could just make out a beautiful, white grand piano standing on a platform inside the shop, waiting for some rich person to buy it. Though which rich person would ever come here to this dark little shop in a narrow, half-forgotten street?

Still, to Luke the strange music shop looked as marvellous as an oasis in the desert to someone dying of thirst. For he, like his dad once had, loved music more than almost anything else. When he was happy, it made him even happier, and when he was sad, it comforted him. He needed it more than ever at the moment.

'If we buy you a new flute,' said his gran, 'you will take care of it, won't you, Luke? You know what happened to the last one...'

Yes, Luke knew what had happened to his old flute – the last present Dad had ever given him.

After Luke's dad had died and Gran had come to live with Luke and his mum, they had moved to a new house with a room especially for Gran. The house was nearer to the city and Luke's mum's work too. Luke had started at a new school. But it was a big, inner-city school – very different from his old one. Before Dad's death, before they moved, Luke had gone to a quiet, country school with a thriving orchestra, where he'd been very happy. Luke's old music teacher had always said that he showed a lot of promise on the flute, and there had been concerts and musicals and plenty of people to hang out with after rehearsals. At night, Luke had practised with his dad, learning to play the piano and keyboard as well. His dad used to perform regularly in musicals and concerts, at weddings and parties, even processions, and Luke had always been allowed to go and watch him at the more exciting events. Luke had practised and played, getting better and better, until he knew that when he grew up he would be a musician like his dad. For a while Luke lived the good life. Then Dad died.

Things went blurry after that. Throughout the funeral, the move, and the lonely black days that followed, music was Luke's friend. But sometimes playing made him sad too, reminding him of happier days of music and fun, and especially of Dad.

Luke's mother was not really musical and now she seemed to resent music altogether. It had taken away her husband, Luke's father, it had changed her life. If only he hadn't worked so hard, if only he hadn't taken on so many gigs and practised so many hours, he might still be there with her.

So she didn't want to hear Luke's music, she hardly seemed to want to know about him at all any more. And although, when she started working full-time, she had at first welcomed Gran and her help, she soon seemed to resent her too, Luke thought, especially Gran's interest in Luke's music. Gran wasn't in his dad's league, but she encouraged Luke and could accompany him on the piano. With Luke's mum always tired, already cross or on the point of losing her temper, Luke found himself turning more and more to his gran, especially with no new friends to help take his mind off things.

The new school was not only very different...it was also very scary. The inner-city kids were tough, streetwise, fast with tongues, feet, hands, ideas. Music was not high on this school's list of priorities. Hard work for exams, results, science, maths and English mattered most to some; sport, especially football, to others; and there were a few whose greatest fun was vandalising anything they could lay hands – or feet – on, and terrorising anyone who looked different.

And Luke did. New boy, pale, sad, thin, always hanging around the virtually unused music block on his own, his head in the clouds. He was an easy target.

Then, just as Luke had resigned himself to a lifetime of nothing ever going right again, a new teacher had arrived. Mr Mezzetti was full of enthusiasm and charisma. He intended to change things at this miserable school that appeared to have no time for poetry, plays or music, extravagant end-of-term shows and concerts. He had started by setting up an orchestra. Of course, Luke had turned up for the first after-school practice. And even though he was the only pupil to come to that first session, Mr Mezzetti had not been daunted. He could see that Luke had talent. Real talent. And since Luke could play so many instruments besides the flute,

Mr Mezzetti quickly decided to build the orchestra around him. They had spent that first after-school practice playing tunes together, with Mr Mezzetti on an electric guitar.

Because Mr Mezzetti was such a bouncy, jolly fellow he soon convinced some other students to join. He told everyone that they'd build up a wonderful, big orchestra playing all kinds of music: classical and modern, jazz and pop. They'd have amazing concerts in the school. More and more students came every week.

Luke had felt a spark of hope ignite inside him then – maybe life could be fun again. When Luke showed Mr Mezzetti his precious flute, the teacher was full of excitement, waving his hands about, his hair standing on end. Luke had always known it was a good one (his dad had only bought the best) but the fact that Mr Mezzetti seemed to feel as passionately as Luke did about his flute made Luke feel that he might have found another ally, like his gran. Luke was almost happy.

But – you mustn't forget the opposition. Ever. And Luke had.

In Luke's class were the cream – if you could call them the cream – of the school, Gobby Jones, Clobber Mackensie and Calum Turner. They had terrorised Luke from the moment he'd arrived, tired and vulnerable, scared stiff of this new, big, grimy school. They were the experts – experts at selecting a victim who looked weak. And their hatred of Luke had just kept on growing, especially when Luke had seemed to forget about them, and their torture of him, momentarily. When his misery had lifted slightly as the orchestra began to take off. So they had set out to get him. That day Luke lost his flute.

They were sorry individuals really – Gobby, Clobber and Cal. They had no hobbies, no skills, no interests. And no one seemed to care about them. No one came to parents' evening to hear how they skipped classes and swore at teachers. No one seemed to expect them home for tea at the end of the day.

So what could they be good at? Where could they show their power? And where could they have fun...?

'Come on, lads! Come on! Look at this wimp! Running home to Mummy after his practice!'

Luke had left behind a sheet of music and gone back into the school to get it after all the other musicians had gone. So he was alone when Gobby, Clobber and Cal ambushed him.

'Mummy's boy with his flutey-wootey, tootle, tootle!'

'No, he's Granny's boy. Sometimes she comes to meet him, tee hee hee!'

'Is he Little Red Riding Hood then, skipping home to Grandma?' cried Gobby, the brains of the gang. 'I know, let's be Big Bad Wolves and gobble him and his flute up!'

'See if he's got any money, first!'

Clobber and Cal held a struggling Luke while Gobby went through his pockets.

'I haven't got any!' cried Luke.

'Don't tell lies. You must be rich if you've got

that silver thing. Nobody ever bought me anything like that. Too expensive. Not that I'd want them to,' Gobby sneered. 'I'm not a wimp.'

He snatched Luke's flute case and snapped it open. The instrument dropped to the ground. Gobby stamped on it with his huge boots. Violence was what Gobby understood best, what he was used to, not music and presents from a dad who was dead but missed. Flutes are tough, but Gobby jumped and jumped on it till it was finished, the keys bent or snapped off. Then the others had a go, for fun.

'Look, he's crying!'

'Wimp! Chicken!'

'And you'd better not tell on us or we'll really do you over next time!'

At last they went, leaving Luke trying to hide his tears and holding a broken and ruined flute.

When Luke had got home, bruised, sore, despairing and disgusted with himself for not doing more to save his beloved flute, his mum demanded to know what had happened. But Luke didn't dare tell her who had wrecked the instrument. He was too scared of them.

She had been angry then. Cold and angry.

'Well, I'm sorry, Luke. You can't have another one. I just can't afford it. You won't tell me who broke it and it's the one your dad gave you. You'll just have to use a school one if you can't take care of your things properly.'

'The school ones are all used up. There are no spares, Mum. There won't be one for me. Oh please, Mum. Please buy—'

'NO! That's enough, Luke. Take better care in future.'

All the misery of losing his dad, and now the flute his dad had given him too, flooded over Luke, overwhelming him with sadness, anger and despair. He ran to his room and shut himself in for the rest of the evening.

Later, as Luke had finally drifted off to sleep, he heard Gran come into his bedroom. 'I'll buy you a flute, Luke,' she whispered, then she tiptoed from his room.

Chapter Three The Music Shop

Far away, the great cathedral bell tolled the hour – five o'clock.

'I hope we're not too late!' Luke cried. 'Come on, Gran. Hurry. Let's go in before the music shop closes.'

But Gran was hesitating on the threshold, as if suddenly reluctant to enter the shop. 'This is the shop I meant, but it seems...different somehow...'

Luke tugged at her hand, 'Perhaps they've redecorated,' he said, as he pushed open the door, though it didn't look like it, with its blistered and flaking paintwork. A bell tinkled as they closed the door behind them and stepped down three dark, wooden steps into the underlit shop. All around them were musical instruments, row upon row of them, of every shape and size: violins, violas, cellos, brass and silver instruments, synthesizers and jazz guitars, drums and cymbals. Then there were shelves of music books, sheet music old and new. In the middle stood the huge, white grand piano, slightly aloft on its platform, a queen among them all.

Luke and his grandmother made their way through the instruments – Luke longing to touch and hold them all – and up to the counter where an old man stood. His beard looked as soft as thistledown. Beside him was a young man with fair, floppy hair, grinning at Luke.

'You're still open, then?' Gran whispered. The silent instruments and the quiet gloom made her speak softly lest she break the spell they seemed to cast. But what kind of spell? she found herself wondering.

'We're always open for those who want to find us.' The old man smiled at Luke invitingly. 'How can I help you, young man?'

'I want…' Luke whispered. The shop waited,

silent, still. 'I want a fl...' he began again – then stopped, for on a dark wall, behind a misty staircase rising up at the back of the shop, something began to glow. How strange. And even as Luke spotted it, the glow grew stronger and more luminous, increasing in power as he looked – yellow, orange, red, scarlet, changing and melting into green and turquoise, purple, lilac, silver and gold.

'That's what I want,' whispered Luke.

'The piccolo?' the old man asked, still smiling.

Luke nodded, breathless. He couldn't speak. He would burst. The colours throbbed and whirled, beckoning to him. It was all too wonderful.

'But I thought we were buying a flute,' said Luke's gran from a million miles away.

Luke wondered how she could doubt his choice. Couldn't she see how wonderful the piccolo was? Couldn't she see it glowing for him?

The old man and the young one exchanged glances.

'Wait a minute!' Luke's grandmother was uneasy. It was silly, she knew, but it seemed to her as if there were shadows in the shop, listening and watching. And Luke's sudden obsession with the strange-looking piccolo on the wall was unsettling. He had never mentioned wanting one before. 'He really wanted a flute, you see...' she added, but her voice faded away as Luke stepped towards the piccolo.

'It *is* a flute, really. Just smaller – it plays an octave higher,' explained the old man. 'Get it down, Leo,' he said, smiling at the younger man behind the counter with him.

'Wait a minute. Are you sure? I don't think you'll be able to play it,' said Gran.

'I can play it. I know I can,' Luke said. Somehow, he knew that the piccolo was meant for him, had been waiting in the shop for him all this time. He just knew. Its changing colours sang to him,

　　　'Take me...

　　　　　'Buy me...

　　　　　　　'Play me...'

Leo took down the piccolo and carried it over to Luke and his gran as if it were the most precious thing in the world, turning it so that Luke could see its engravings of twists and curls and leaves and flowers. It was so small, so neat, so wonderfully made.

Luke took it and held his breath. The colours faded gently away, leaving the piccolo silver and beautiful. Luke suddenly felt as if he could do anything. He itched to play the instrument.

'It's very old,' explained the old man.

'Yes,' said Gran. 'I can see that.'

'A one-off. Never been another quite like it.'

'Where did it come from?'

'It's been here a long time, Madam.'

'It'll be expensive then?'

'Priceless.' Leo grinned again. His hair was floppy and straight, but his smile was curly.

'Have you another one that's more…ordinary?' Gran asked. But it wasn't the price that bothered her. Somehow, everything about the piccolo was so strange, it almost…frightened her.

'Only this one.'

'Then we'll have to leave it. I'm sorry.'

Luke's gran turned to go, heading hurriedly towards the door.

But Luke's pleading voice stopped her.

'Gran, I want this piccolo more than anything else in the whole world. Please, please, please, Gran!'

'Why not just try it out. There's a little room upstairs. Just try it. You'd like to have a go, wouldn't you, Luke?' Leo asked. 'Then you can see if it's really what you want, and set your gran's mind at rest that you can play it.'

Luke nodded and as he did so he felt a tingling sensation run from the piccolo up his arm and then all over his body, leaving a feeling of familiarity behind, as if he had known and played the instrument many times before.

Leo led Luke over to the dark wooden stairs with a strip of worn red carpet running up their centre. Gran followed them as they climbed.

And it seemed that all the musical instruments watched them on their way.

Chapter Four Black Cat Dancing

Leo took them up the stairs, which turned round a corner and then another corner, until at last they reached a door. It opened into a smallish square room with panelled walls and wooden floorboards, bare except for a square window and a square cupboard.

'You'll be all right here.' He smiled and closed the door quietly behind him, leaving Luke and his grandmother standing in the middle of this box of a room.

Luke stroked the silver shine of the piccolo, lifted it to his lips, then lowered it again. In the room's stillness, only the piccolo's engraved flowers and leaves seemed to move. Luke's gran waited.

'Don't watch me!' he said softly. 'I can't play if you watch me.'

His gran turned to the window and opened it. Light and air entered the room. 'Oh!' she exclaimed. 'It's wonderful. Look!'

They were high above the city. Below them stretched a very old garden full of tall grasses, reeds, brambles, nettles and weeds, with roses, roses, roses, red, pink and white, growing over everything like a cloak. The garden rose to a high red brick wall with a pattern on it. Leaning out of the window she could see the bridges, the river and the quay and beyond them fields and trees, now turning red and yellow in the hot September sun. The trees stretched up to the purple of the great moor to the north of the city.

That was in the distance. On a little green bank in the garden just below, a black cat was curled up, fast asleep.

'Look, Luke,' Gran said again.

But Luke wasn't interested. He was breathing down the piccolo to warm it, feeling its smallness, its daintiness. Gently, gently, he stroked the piccolo. In his mind for a moment he saw his old flute lying shattered and ruined on the ground.

I'll take care of *you*. I won't let them wreck *you*, he thought. And blew his first note.

Eeek! Squeak! Sparrow notes.

A deep breath. He knew he could do this. Luke blew again. Then, high, clear and strong came a note that nearly sent him through the ceiling and out of the window. A note of such piercing sweetness that it made the whole room quiver and shiver…

and tremble…

and rock…

And then…a tiny sound, so perfect that it seemed to melt into the air around it. More notes followed, strong, loud, not squeaking, until suddenly, out of nowhere, came a melody of unbelievable purity. It had the perfume of roses, a touch of velvet, the smile of a beautiful girl, a taste of honey. All the senses caught and held in those notes singing high and loud and clear – perfect piccolo notes. Not a squeaky sparrow any more, but an eagle of music soaring in the sky, up to the blue heavens above the clouds, reaching out for the golden sun.

Luke could only hold on for the ride for it seemed as if he wasn't playing the piccolo at all. It felt like it was playing him. He saw his gran turn, astonished, from the open window. The room had been transformed into a shining world of music.

Luke didn't want to stop. Ever. He moved towards the window, still playing, and imagined the notes flying out past the roofs and chimneys. He imagined some notes floating down into the wild garden with its green bank where the black cat lay sleeping.

And ever so slowly the cat lifted up its head and stretched its legs and its paws, arching its furry back, waving its tail till it was higher than its head. Last of all, it opened its pink mouth with its sharp white teeth, in a huge yawn, and twitched its whiskers till they zinged. Then, as light and dainty as the notes in the air, the little cat seemed to dance, lifting its paws one after another, then standing on its back legs, waving its paws in the air, leaping and stretching after a tortoiseshell butterfly that flew and flitted near by. Even the flowers and grasses of the garden swayed and shimmered in time to the music.

As he played on, Luke knew that it was the piccolo that had brought him here to the strange shop and that he had to take it home with him.

A knock at the door.

'Made a decision yet?' asked Leo, opening it.

Gran shook her head slightly. She felt almost overwhelmed by the playing. 'Let's go downstairs now, Luke,' she said.

The music died away slowly. Luke lowered the piccolo from his mouth and stood looking at it as if he was emerging from a dream, or broken spell. Was he awake or asleep? He couldn't tell any more.

Luke's grandmother closed the window. The cat had disappeared, the garden was still and the square room ordinary once more. Slowly, Luke and his gran followed Leo down the stairs, back into the gloomy shop.

Luke tugged at her sleeve. 'Please, Gran. Please buy it for me.'

'I'm still not sure. Something feels rather...strange. I've never heard you play like that. I've never heard anyone...not even your father...' Gran looked at Luke carefully. 'It has to be this instrument, doesn't it? You've decided for some reason.'

Luke nodded.

'Well,' she shook herself, 'OK, you can have it. I'm sure I'm being silly anyway. It sounded beautiful.'

'It's right for him, Madam,' said the old man. 'And we like people to have the instrument that's right for them. Don't worry, it won't be too expensive for you.'

Five minutes later they walked out of the shop, Luke clutching his piccolo in its silk-lined case. Together they made their way back up cobbled, sloping Shadow Lane. As they turned into the bright high street Gran looked back. But the shop and Shadow Lane were hidden in mist.

Chapter Five Evening Encounter

Luke and his grandmother heard the cathedral bells ring out six o'clock as they hurried home, Luke walking on air, clutching the piccolo in its handsome black and silver case, his grandmother pleased with his happiness and yet with a slightly uneasy feeling that she couldn't shake off. She was sure everything was fine but… But she couldn't help wishing they'd bought a good, ordinary flute instead. Because, well, she didn't really know, but everything in the shop had been so weird, so…peculiar. She hoped it would all turn out well for her beloved grandson – he'd had such a bad time lately. In the meantime, she needed to get home to cook some tea. Lately, Luke's mother didn't seem to care if they ate anything or not.

Gran smiled at Luke's happiness, so rare these days. He was even humming to himself, a strange little tune. She'd heard the tune before, she realised. It was the one Luke had played on the piccolo in the odd box of a room, with the beautiful view outside and the little cat dancing...

'Oh, Luke, look, look!'

'What? Look at what?'

'The black cat crossing the road. I'm sure it's the one I saw out of the window at the music shop. The one that looked like it was dancing to your playing.'

'Oh, Gran, don't be silly. It's a perfectly ordinary black cat. There are lots of them about.'

Luke spoke gently. He hoped Gran was all right. That strange shop must have got to her even more than it had to him. Already, in the early evening light and bustle of the high street, the overwhelming sense of calling he had felt when he saw and held the piccolo for the first time was fading. It was simply the excitement of seeing such a beautifully-made instrument that had gone to his head, he told himself. And of course, such a well-made instrument would make his playing sound better than normal. He couldn't wait to get home and try it again.

'And Gran,' Luke added, 'cats don't dance, you know.'

But before she could answer, Gobby Jones shot up in front of them, jack-in-the-box style, grinning evilly, eyes glinting,

'Well, well, if it isn't Lukey. Been shopping with Granny, then? Bought a lovely new tootle-tootle?'

Clobber and Cal pushed up behind him, blocking the pavement. They were smiling too, but not pleasantly.

Luke clutched the piccolo to his chest. He didn't know where they'd suddenly appeared from. He'd forgotten them and everything else awful in his life for a moment, he'd been so happy. But now they stood on the pavement in front of him, reminding him of everything bad he had managed to forget.

'Excuse us, please. We want to go past,' said Luke's grandmother. She smiled uncertainly at the boys. Were these friends of Luke's? They didn't seem to be the sort of boys he used to hang around with.

'Better look after this new tootle-tootle,' grinned Cal. 'It mustn't get busted like the ovver one, eh, Gran?'

'It's bad he don't tek good care of his gear,' muttered Clobber.

'Don't get your bloomers in a twist, Gran,' laughed Gobby, with his terrific talent for truly horrible, vile words, even when he sounded like he was being polite. 'We'll take care of that bit of cheap tin for him, won't we, lads?'

Then they ran off sniggering. As fast as they'd appeared, they'd gone.

Anger came bubbling up inside Luke, like the build-up inside a volcano before it explodes. He wanted to hurt Gobby and his gang, kick them, stamp on them, treat them as they had treated his flute. Then he heard his grandmother say quietly, 'Friends?' She lifted her eyebrows.

'Um, yeah! Sort of. They're always joking around.' What else could he say? He couldn't tell her the truth. He was too ashamed. Hadn't he just stood there and let them threaten him, and his piccolo, again, and not done a thing?

Something in Gran's eyes told Luke she didn't believe him. Not really. But she didn't say anything more about it, just smiled at him and they hurried home.

Chapter Six Strange Sounds

Luke showed Mum the piccolo when they got in. He knew there was no point – she wouldn't be pleased for him – but he tried anyway.

'Very nice,' she said. 'Gran spoils you. Mind you take better care of it than the last one,' she added.

Luke's shoulders slumped, but Gran grinned at him over her shoulder as she headed for the kitchen. Gran was always on his side.

Luke took the piccolo out of its case so that his mum could look at it properly.

She sniffed a bit. 'It looks very expensive,' she said. 'I hope Gran didn't spend too much money on you. And why did you buy this? I thought you were getting a flute.'

It shone and sang to me in the shop and it seemed to want me to buy it, Luke thought to himself, but didn't say. Aloud he answered, 'I just liked the look of it and when I played it, it did sound great. Ask Gran.'

Suddenly his mother smiled – she was in a good mood tonight, for once. 'Where did you get it from?'

'The music shop in Shadow Lane.'

'Oh, I know. The old part of the town. The Council talked of pulling it down some time ago, but something stopped them, I don't know what.'

'Mum?' Luke knew he was pushing his luck, but she did seem to be in a better mood than usual and it would mean so much to him. 'Can I play the piccolo for you?'

'No!' she snapped, then, 'I mean, no – you've got homework to do. What have you got tonight?'

'Maths and science.'

'Well, get on with that. You've got to earn your living when you grow up, and proper subjects like those will help. Not music.'

'Dad earned his living with music,' Luke tried defiantly.

'Yes, and see where that got him. And me.'

Miserably, Luke got on with his homework in his room, but he worked as fast as he could. As soon as he was finished, he opened the piccolo case again and picked up the instrument. After this evening with his run in with Gobby and the argument with his mum, Luke felt he needed to play – to clear his head and make himself feel better. Still, he found himself breathing hard. He felt nervous. And what if his mum was in one of those moods where she wouldn't even let him practise in his room with the door shut. When the sound of an instrument, any instrument at all, would make her complain of a headache and insist on complete silence for the rest of the evening. He couldn't bear it, he had to play.

But when he blew the first note of his tune – the special piccolo melody that had written itself in his brain – the singing notes soared happily into the air, shining colours of sound, sweeter than honey, smoother than ice cream, a tender melody that seemed to come from long ago. It seemed to rise up into the room, into the air and out of the window, open because of the heat of the day, the golden melody blowing and melting into the silver birch tree outside whose leaves were turning yellow-gold.

When Luke looked away from the window, still playing, his mother was there. She had halted, still as a statue, inside his bedroom doorway, half-turned to where Luke was playing. Tears were rolling down her cheeks.

Without thinking, Luke stopped playing and went to hug her, but just before his arms could reach around her for the mother's comfort that he still sought, she shook her head and rubbed the back of her hand across her eyes. 'I'm fine, Luke,' she said quickly. 'Get on with your practice if you must.' And she left the room, shutting the door behind her.

Luke stood for a moment, his arms hanging

lifelessly at his sides. Then he turned back to his piccolo, for one last tune before bed. This time he found himself thinking about tomorrow at school. He'd show Mr Mezzetti the piccolo and play it for him. He was sure that Mr Mezzetti would love it, even if his mum didn't.

The room was turning dark now as the sun set outside. Thinking of school reminded Luke of Gobby and his gang and his earlier anger suddenly surged again inside him. He didn't want to think of them. He had better things to do, didn't he? He mustn't think about them. He must *not*! He raised the piccolo to his lips again.

He blew.

But everything was different.

The notes came out like a curse, sour not sweet, harsh not melodic, cruel not comforting, hating not loving, fierce, aggressive, violent, angry. But he couldn't stop playing.

At first Luke was confused. He didn't know what was happening. Then he was terrified.

His world was turning upside down again. He wanted to stop, but for a moment he couldn't. His arms wouldn't move, his bottom lip seemed frozen to the mouthpiece. He had to go on playing. Playing musical horrors he didn't want to hear.

Let me go! He concentrated with all his power. Let me go! Please!

The music stopped. The piccolo released him. Luke fell back, exhausted, but as he did so the room went completely dark, shutting out the last of the evening sunshine. It was as if a shadow had slipped through the cracks around the bedroom door and into the room with him. He shivered. What had changed his beautiful music into something sinister and shadowy, looming and threatening in the corner? Luke felt darkness building up all around him, full of terror and fear, the stuff of nightmares.

'No!' Luke whispered desperately. 'Let me go! Please!' He didn't know who he was talking to, if anyone at all, but suddenly the street lamp outside came on, lighting up the room. The shadows seemed to slip away, silently. Trembling, Luke laid the piccolo on his small bedside table. Its engraved leaves and flowers shone in the light from the street.

It's so pretty, thought Luke, so harmless. I was only afraid of it because I was tired, he told himself. Maybe I even fell asleep without realising it, and it was all a nightmare brought on by worrying about Gobby and his gang. After all, I love my piccolo. Luke yawned. So tired. Such a strange, weird day. Sleep now… And Luke fell asleep watching the piccolo change and glow in his line of vision.

In the hallway, Luke's grandmother finally moved away from Luke's bedroom door, heading back to her own room. She had stopped to listen to Luke's playing too, just as his mother had done earlier. But not for the same reasons. Not because the piccolo moved her, because it frightened her. It frightened her a lot.

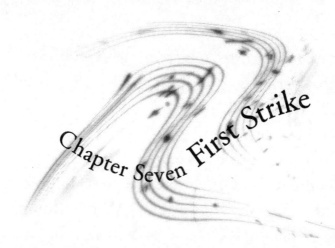

At lunch break the next day at school, Mr Mezzetti admired the piccolo just as Luke had thought he would. The nightmares of the day and evening before were forgotten as Luke shared in his teacher's delight with his new instrument. Mr Mezzetti said that it was one of the oldest wind instruments he'd ever seen, that the engravings of flowers and leaves on it were wonderful. It had even given him an idea for the concert he wanted the students to perform at the end of term. The school orchestra was big enough now for Mr Mezzetti to have a whole programme of songs, solos, pieces and groups planned, and now he would add a short musical play as well, pieces from *Peter and the Wolf,* with the piccolo performing the part of the bird, instead of a flute.

He bounced away, beaming and thinking of more ideas for his concert, the first the school had had in years. He left Luke to practise in the music block. Luke found himself playing the same tune again, the one that seemed to have popped into his head from nowhere the first time he played the piccolo. He felt he was getting to know it really well now – and he introduced some variations. There were a few other kids from the orchestra hanging around and some of them – led by a girl called Zoe, whom Luke had walked home with a few times after rehearsals, as she lived quite near him – congratulated him. He liked Zoe, he hoped she might become a friend. Perhaps now she had heard him on the piccolo she would be more impressed by him. His playing was good, he could admit that to himself. He might be a wimp – with no friends and a mum who didn't even seem to like him – but at least he could play. Though perhaps not quite as remarkably as he had imagined yesterday, in the mysterious gloom of that strange shop!

At the end of the lunch hour they went back to their classrooms. Luke walked with Zoe, who was making terrific progress on the drums. Zoe was a tall, happy girl, older than Luke, and she made him feel safe. When she left him to go to her different classroom Luke hummed his little tune as he turned the corner to join his own class, holding the piccolo case safely.

They were waiting for him. Lined up. Gobby, Clobber and Cal.

Luke looked around desperately. Surely there was someone nearby who could help him? But no, Zoe had disappeared and the others had already gone inside. There he was, stuck, alone with his enemies and panic. He tried to run but it was no good. They encircled him easily. He clutched the precious piccolo to his chest.

'Still got that titchy bit of old rubbish with

you, eh, Pukey-Lukey?' Gobby grinned.

Clobber joined in. 'Thought you'd have got sommat bigger and better by now. Sommat a proper size.'

'Some kids say it's valuable though, even if it's tiny,' murmured Gobby.

'Your old dear must be rich buying you sommat like that,' Cal added his bit.

'Let me go. We'll all be late for lessons!' cried Luke. He knew he sounded feeble, but what could he do, three to one, and all so much bigger than him? Anger bubbled up inside him. Why should he be bullied by these horrible kids? He'd done nothing to them. And why was he pathetic enough to just take it? Why couldn't he stand up to them?

'Lessons are boring anyway. This is much more fun,' Clobber said.

'Leave me alone!' cried Luke. 'Let me go. Please.' As he said these words, he realised how familiar they seemed. But before he could think any further on it, Cal grabbed the piccolo case.

'Let's look at this old bit of tin whistle,' he said.

'Don't you dare! Don't you dare touch it!' By now Luke was ballistic with rage, yet he knew he wouldn't have the nerve to do anything, even if Cal started on his piccolo too.

'Or what? What can you do, chicken legs?' Cal laughed like a drain as he spat on his hands, then smeared them all over the case. Luke reached for it pleadingly, just as Mr Bates, the maths teacher, walked round the corner. Gobby, Cal and Clobber vanished like a puff of – no, not smoke, sulphur. Luke found himself alone again, but at least the piccolo case and piccolo were safely back in his hands.

'Come along, Luke,' said Mr Bates, 'or you'll be late for our maths lesson. You ready for it?'

Luke's head throbbed with pain and anger as he hurried after Mr Bates into class.

That day, when school finished, he joined up with Zoe and her friend Ellie to walk home with them. They didn't seem to mind him tagging along, though he was sure they were just being nice. But Zoe was the kind of girl no one ever bullied. They wouldn't dream of it. Luke would be safe with her, for the moment. They wouldn't dare harm the piccolo with Zoe around.

That evening, homework finished, Luke hurried his piano and keyboard practice, then dashed up to his room and got the precious piccolo out of its case. This was *the* moment of the day.

He rubbed the case carefully with a soft cloth, to remove any trace of horrible Cal and his loathsome spit. How dare he pollute it?

'I hope he catches the plague and is covered with red spots – all filled with yellow goo that oozes out of them,' Luke muttered angrily to himself as he prepared to hear the beautiful melody he now knew so well.

But...*scream, scritch, screech*, nails scraping down a blackboard, the roar of a pneumatic drill, all combined in a horrible noise that hurt and made every hair on Luke's head stand on end. Suddenly he was boiling hot, then freezing cold, trembling as he was drenched with icy, sticky sweat. Luke tried to take the piccolo away from his mouth but there was no power in his hands. The harsh sounds poured out of the instrument relentlessly, cruelly, polluting the air around him.

In the corner of Luke's room a shadow began to form. It seemed, momentarily, to take on the shape of a nightmare figure, elongated and hideous. Luke tried to cower away from it, though as soon as he saw it, it was gone again. And still Luke couldn't stop playing. It seemed there was no power in him to stop. The piccolo had all the power. Then, suddenly, his will to stop playing seemed to win through at last and Luke found he was able to lower the piccolo from his mouth.

'Luke! Whatever was that horrible noise?'

His mother stood in the doorway, his gran behind her, both of them horrified.

'You know about my headaches. You know how bad they get. How could you make such a racket?' Luke's mum shouted at him.

She didn't hear Gran, her face pale and worried, whisper, 'It's not Luke. It's that piccolo somehow. I'm sure of it.'

Luke felt dazed. 'I'm sorry,' he said. 'I don't know—'

'Just go to bed, Luke. You're driving me mad!' His mum stormed from the room.

'Luke, darling,' his gran tried. 'Shall I take that away for now?' She reached cautiously for the piccolo.

'No!' Luke pulled it tight to him. 'It was my fault, don't take it away from me. Please.' Without it he wouldn't be able to play his beautiful tune so well, without it he would be nothing, then no one would congratulate him, no one would even notice him at school. It was his fault he had played badly that evening, it had to be.

So Gran went reluctantly away, without the piccolo, and Luke climbed into bed too exhausted to think, and slept a dreamless sleep.

*

Next day it was all over the school that Cal had arrived that morning and then collapsed going into Assembly. He was found to be covered in huge red boils, oozing yellow pus, and was rushed away to hospital as fast as possible. No one as yet knew what was wrong or what had caused it...

Chapter Eight Second Strike

Luke went through the school morning, stunned. He didn't know what to think, what to believe. All around him he could hear talk of measles, chicken pox, illness and infections. Would they close the school? Gossip was everywhere, the kids high on rumour and terror, real and imagined. Luke wanted to talk to someone about his own fears. Could it be…? Had *he* caused Cal's illness by wishing it on him? Was his willpower as strong as that? Or…was it the power of the piccolo that had given Cal those aching, oozing boils? No, that was silly. There was nothing wrong with his perfect piccolo! It was all coincidence. Besides, Luke told himself, he should just enjoy it. Cal deserved everything bad that happened to him – he was a cruel, mean, vandalising bully. And yet, and yet, Luke felt guilty somehow. Even if common sense told him that Cal's condition was nothing to do with him or the piccolo, as Luke made his way through the school day he couldn't shake the feeling of guilt.

At least Cal was out of his way. In the circumstances, Luke thought Gobby and Clobber wouldn't bother him much either. So he settled to his work and the day rolled on steadily and safely.

At the end of school, Luke went along to the music room. He was early and no one else had arrived for rehearsals yet. The September sun streamed in through the windows, filling the room with golden light. Luke wanted to play and enjoy the piccolo on its own, before the others came and he had to become part of the orchestra. And perhaps he wanted to prove to himself how normal his instrument really was, though he would barely admit that to himself. He moved past the drums, guitars and keyboards over to one of the windows overlooking the playground. He opened his bag and took out the beautiful object that he'd kept out of sight and danger during the day. Standing in a bright shaft of sunshine, he lifted the piccolo to play. At the sound of his first notes, the dust particles in the air shimmered and danced all around like bits of thistledown or tiny elves. The music sounded beautiful and Luke sighed a breath of relief as he played on. Of course it did – what did he expect?

But several bars into his piccolo tune, Luke saw someone coming back into the playground, although school was finished. It was Clobber in his huge boots, twisting his head round, searching for something, frowning when he didn't see it. Then he looked upwards and saw Luke at the window. His face screwed up into a mask of hate, he shook his fist and stabbed rudely at Luke with his fingers.

'I 'ate you,' he mouthed, 'and that junk you've got there. I'm coming in to git you and I'll break you and it in two.'

Luke felt his breath quicken with fear. He

tried to keep playing softly and gently to calm his fear. But suddenly the horror began again.

The notes slurred and blurred as if struggling through oozing, stinking mud. Then they dragged themselves from the slow stickiness, going faster and faster till they spun and whirled like desert sand, obliterating air, stopping breathing. A terrible screeching sound.

The beautiful thistledown dust particles fled out of the shafts of sunlight and into the rest of the room. Drawing darkness with it, slid a shadow. A changing, distorted, evil shape, blotting out the sun. It seemed almost to have a form, seemed to dance with jerky movements towards Luke, its arms outstretched. Luke tried to restrain the piccolo, to alter what it was playing and make the shadow disappear. Then he was distracted again by Clobber.

Outside, Clobber was still mouthing and pulling faces at him. If only he would go away like Cal, Luke found himself thinking. Words rang inside his head: I don't want any of this! I don't deserve it. Stop it all! Save me! Let me be happy.

And suddenly Tom Thompson, head boy, the biggest and strongest boy in the school, captain of the football and cricket team, strode into the playground.

Yes, let him deal with Clobber. The thought went through Luke's head before he was even aware of it. But as the piccolo played on screechily, Luke watched fascinated, hypnotised, as Tom advanced on Clobber. Luke could barely hear the music he was playing now, or see the shadow that curled around him. All he could think about was what was about to happen.

Putting both hands on Clobber's shoulders, Tom Thompson pushed the bully over, then placed one large football boot on Clobber's chest and held him down so he couldn't move. Clobber wriggled uselessly, his face no longer a mask of hate, but of terror. He banged and thrashed about, but it was hopeless. The foot stayed put and Clobber couldn't shift it. Tom seemed to push down harder and Clobber groaned with pain then started shouting for help. Luke felt a thrill of triumph spread through him – it was good to see Clobber on the receiving end of bullying for once. He blew harder into the piccolo and the high, tortured notes came even faster.

By now, a crowd of excited students had rushed across the playground, leaving their after-school clubs and practices to see what the commotion was about. Some of them carried instruments – they'd been on their way to orchestra practise when the unfolding scene had distracted them. They blocked Luke's view and as his enemy disappeared from sight, Luke found himself released from the piccolo. The terrible music stopped and the room returned to bright sunlight. For a moment, Luke looked about him, dazed. Then, quickly, he put the piccolo in its bag and rushed out to the playground.

What was going on? What had happened to Clobber? Luke joined the ever-growing throng just as the head teacher and Mrs Hancock, the PE teacher, arrived.

'What were you doing? What were you

thinking of?' demanded the head, glaring furiously at Tom Thompson as he pulled him away from Clobber. 'You're always so responsible. Whatever happened?'

He helped the weeping Clobber to his feet.

Tom seemed to be coming out of a kind of trance, but he still looked confused. At last he said, 'I don't know... I can't think... Something came over me... Told me to...'

'I didn't do nothing to him. He just ran at me and knocked me down!' Clobber howled. 'He hurt me!'

'Come with me,' said Mrs Hancock. 'I'll clean you up a bit and see if there's anything wrong.'

'You,' said the head teacher to Tom. 'Go and wait outside my office. I want to find out what happened.'

'I don't know what happened,' moaned Tom, as he headed off in the direction of the head's office.

Luke spotted Zoe in the gathered crowd and went over to join her. He pretended not to know what had happened, but inside he was in turmoil. He couldn't make believe it was coincidence any more. Somehow the piccolo had made Tom Thompson bully Clobber, and it had done it for Luke. For a moment, Luke felt guilty again, but then he remembered Clobber's scared face. How that had made him want to smile with triumph at the time. Had the piccolo really got revenge on Clobber because he had willed it to? Shouldn't he be grateful then?

But what about the elusive, fearsome shadow? Luke could deny the existence of it no longer. How did that ghostly apparition fit into the strange thing Luke's life had now become? It frightened him, but why should it? It was on his side after all, wasn't it?

Luke shook himself from his wonderings to see Gobby, among the other kids, staring at him, eyes slitted, curious and wondering. With a lurch of his stomach, Luke remembered that Gobby was clever. Would he guess something about what was going on? But then, did it matter if he did? Luke was safe now. He had his magic piccolo to protect him.

Chapter Nine Third Strike

Back at home that evening, Luke felt very odd, very alive and *very* aware of strange things going on around him, undercurrents of fear and…triumph. Luke had no idea what had really happened but he was beginning to realise the power of the piccolo. It seemed that it could hear Luke's thoughts, feel his anger and fear, but it could act on them as Luke had failed to. It made him stronger then?

Luke was too restless to finish his tea and his mother grumbled, telling him not to waste good food and to be grateful for what he was given. To escape, Luke went up to his room to play his piccolo. He felt half afraid of it, but he was half addicted too, and when he saw the case he could not resist getting the instrument out, looking at it and putting it to his lips. Would the notes he played be beautiful or ugly, kind or cruel?

This time, the sounds were harmonious, serene, as pleasant as the warm and golden September day outside. Luke felt as happy as his tune sounded.

His gran knocked on the door and came in. Luke stopped playing.

'That was lovely, Luke.' She sat on his bed. 'Are things...are things a bit better for you now?' she said suddenly.

What did she mean, 'better for you now'? Did she know about the piccolo and what it had done to Gobby's gang? No, she couldn't. But should he tell her?

'Gran...this piccolo...'

'Yes, Luke? Is there something bothering you about it...?'

She seemed to Luke to take a sharp breath in and momentarily narrow her eyes in the instrument's direction.

What if she doesn't understand and she takes it away from me, Luke thought suddenly. He couldn't bear to be without it now. It brought him attention and praise. It protected him. 'No, nothing…it's great…' Not used to keeping secrets from his gran, Luke rambled on guiltily. 'It's just…er…I've got a massive part in the school show. Do you think I'll play all right if I practise lots? Will I be ready in time, do you think?'

Gran nodded slowly. 'I know you'll do what's right when the time comes,' she said and went quietly away. Luke couldn't help feeling that she wasn't talking about the show. He finished his homework and his practice and went to bed. He felt very tired.

When Luke left the house next day, he felt no surprise that Gobby was waiting at the gate.

'What do you want?' Luke asked.

'I want to know what you did to Cal and Clobber!'

'What do you mean?' Luke panicked. Could

Gobby have worked it out so quickly?

'I saw you at the window, blowing that tin whistle like crazy and watching while Clobber got beaten up. I reckon it had something to do with you. Everyone knows Tom Thompson is usually a goody-goody. Did you pay him to have a go at Clobber or something?' Gobby advanced menacingly. 'Ever since you got that piece of tin rubbish you've been acting even weirder than before. And I don't think Cal's disease came out of nowhere either. You probably bought some freaky potion and gave it to him somehow.'

Luke was relieved that Gobby hadn't worked out the whole truth, but he was still in trouble. 'No I—'

'So with all this cash to chuck around,' Gobby went on, 'you can get some more from that rich old dear of yours for me, or I'm going to the head teacher with my suspicions.'

'But you can't prove I did anything!'

'No, but I can stir up trouble for you. Lots of it, Pukey-face. And I can always take that piccolo as down payment if you're not ready with the readies! Be by the school gates first thing at lunchtime, or else. They'll all be at lunch so no one will be about. And don't try any of your funny tricks on me!'

Then he ran off down the street. He might have been laughing, but his eyes were angry, his face wild. He's crazy, thought Luke. What will he do to me? The piccolo, he thought next. The piccolo will save me.

But Gobby scared Luke, he scared him the most out of the three bullies. Suddenly, faced with Gobby, Luke doubted if even the piccolo could save him. On frightened legs, he made his way to school.

The news at school was that Cal was recovering, but had to stay in hospital for a while, and that Clobber was missing from school and couldn't be found anywhere, even by Gobby. Luke thought of finding Mr Mezzetti and telling him everything about being bullied but found he couldn't. Luke felt sure that such a friendly, happy, strong person as Mr Mezzetti would just wonder why Luke didn't stand up for himself. So he was too ashamed to tell him.

Perhaps he should go to the head teacher before Gobby did. But what was he going to say? He didn't know what lies – or truths – Gobby had thought up about him.

Luke had no answers to his problems, but he did know the answers to his work so he got on with that instead. But throughout lessons, Gobby's eyes watched Luke, like a snake watching a rabbit.

At lunchtime, in total misery, Luke walked to the school gates to meet Gobby. In his bag he carried a five-pound note, that he'd nipped home and taken from his holiday savings, and the piccolo, safely tucked away at the bottom. Dawdling on the way, he could see Gobby lounging by the gates already, hands in pockets, grinning as Luke walked towards him.

Suddenly, the sight of Gobby's gloating face was more than Luke could take. Anger pushed out to replace his fear. He pulled the piccolo from his bag, fished it out of its case, not handling it lovingly for once, but snatching it fiercely, angrily, full of hate and madness.

And he played the piccolo melody.

But it was so different again. Shrill and sharp. The blue sky darkened. A black cloud raced suddenly over the school and the trees and bushes at the gates. And out of the cloud's shade emerged something thin, elongated, horrible – the Shadow. In the shape of a misshapen man. He had come. Luke felt a sneering laugh bubble up inside him.

A car was approaching the school, going faster than it should. The school gates were open when they would normally have been closed. The piccolo played on wildly, Luke had barely to do anything. Gobby looked about in confusion at the sudden darkness and Luke's erratic playing. For a moment Luke felt wonderful...until he suddenly saw what was going to happen.

Stop! Please stop! He meant both the car and the piccolo – stop, please! Let me go! I didn't mean this! But the piccolo wasn't doing what

Luke wished for after all. It seemed to have a will of its own. This time he couldn't stop playing however hard he tried. No, it was the piccolo – *it* wouldn't stop, even when Luke begged it to.

Gobby, get out of the way! Look out! Jump! Jump!

The car's tyres squealed across the tarmac.

Luke tried to stop playing, or to get to Gobby and push him to safety, but his lip was stuck to the piccolo's mouthpiece, his fingers rampaging on the keys like robots from hell that could not be halted.

And now Luke could see the demon face of the shadow shape behind the wheel, its mouth a dark space that widened into a black, grinning hole, directed at Luke. At last Gobby had turned to run. Too late, surely. Luke shut his eyes. He couldn't bear to look.

'This isn't me! I don't want to kill him! I just want him to leave me alone. Please, Piccolo, Shadow, whatever you are, please stop! You're frightening me! *Stop!*

Chapter Ten Unlikely Friend

Luke opened his eyes. The piccolo dangled from one limp hand. His shouting must have broken the spell at last, he realised, his terrified voice breaking through and tearing the piccolo from his mouth. But it had been so hard to do this time. His body was so tired that he felt like sinking to the ground where he stood.

But he couldn't. He had to check on Gobby. How was he? Was he...dead? A crowd of younger children had arrived. They had heard the squeal of the speeding car's tyres and come running. Then the head teacher and the deputy, Mrs Gilpin, appeared, pushing through the crowd.

'What's happened? What's going on?'

Luke followed them through the crowd, frightened of what he might see at its centre. Gobby was on the floor, almost hysterical…but he was alive and OK.

'It only just missed me! I could've been killed!' Gobby shrieked.

Mrs Gilpin bent down to comfort him.

'What happened?' demanded the head teacher.

'A car. I was just walking along and *whoosh* – this car came whizzing straight for me. I only just managed to get out of the way in time, Sir. Sir, it meant to kill me!' Then Gobby spotted Luke standing behind the head teacher and his already white face suddenly looked even more ghostly. But to Luke's surprise Gobby didn't say anything more, didn't give him away.

The headteacher appealed to the children gathered around. 'Did any of you see anything?' he asked.

'We saw the car,' said one. 'It came out of nowhere and headed straight for Gobby.'

'But we didn't see anyone driving it,' said another.

'Strange things do seem to be happening at the school at the moment,' said Mrs Gilpin as she helped Gobby to his feet. 'One boy catches a mystery illness, another is attacked by the head prefect for no reason and a third is almost knocked down by an out-of-control car, apparently driverless.'

'Where is the car, by the way?' asked the head.

But although no one had seen the car leave through the school gates, after it missed Gobby, it was nowhere to be seen.

For Luke, the rest of the school day passed as if in a dream – or a nightmare. Now he knew that the piccolo wasn't magical, it was more…haunted, possessed. By that Shadow! It showed the same feelings of anger and hostility that Luke felt himself. And it didn't give him power at all, it merely used Luke for its own angry ends. The piccolo itself, or the Shadow from within it, was a bully! It had twisted and manipulated Luke's own emotions. Yes, he was angry with Gobby and his gang, but he was more angry with himself for being too pathetic to stand up to or ignore them. He didn't want anyone dead! He didn't want to become a bully himself, hurting others – frightening Clobber so much that he ran away from school, getting straight guys like Tom Thompson into trouble, even making someone so sick that they were in hospital. But how could he escape? The Shadow's power seemed to get stronger every time he played the piccolo. What could he do with it, to keep it safely away from people? What was the cause of its evil power? And who – or what – was the Shadow exactly?

Gran said I'd know the right thing to do, Luke thought, but I don't. He longed to talk to someone about it all. Mr Mezzetti? Zoe? They wouldn't believe him. They'd probably think he was crazy. He wanted Zoe to become a real friend – this would only frighten her off. He couldn't tell his mother, she'd just dismiss it as rubbish. He needed to talk to Gran. She would understand. She would be able to help.

Luke's maths teacher interrupted his worries, to tell him off for daydreaming. For a moment, Luke glared crossly at the teacher, then he stopped himself. He must be very careful. Something might happen. Suppose his mum told him off, as she did nearly every day now, and he got angry? Would the Shadow attack her?

So far dreadful things only happened when he played the piccolo and the Shadow appeared – but suppose the Shadow somehow managed to escape the piccolo and attach itself to him? For always. It did seem to be getting stronger, more independent of Luke's piccolo playing every time it appeared. And maybe next time Luke wouldn't be able to stop it.

Suddenly Luke knew what he had to do. He had to get rid of the piccolo, much as he loved it and what it did for his playing. But he couldn't throw it away. No, someone else might find it and discover its dreadful power. He knew he couldn't destroy it – it still meant too much to him, despite everything. He couldn't even risk getting his gran involved. He didn't want her to be harmed in any way. There was really only one answer. He had to take it back to the shop. He must return it to the strange place that it had come from.

But…but…he didn't want to do this on his own. He was scared, no, terrified. His suppressed fear of, and anger towards, his tormentors had landed him in a far worse terror.

At last the afternoon ended. Luke got the piccolo out, stroking it once more – it was so beautiful, so dear to him because, in a way, it had done so much for him, something so small, but so dangerous. A tear trickled down his face as he put the instrument back in its case and then into his school bag. Speaking to no one, he hurried to the gate.

Gobby was there – he looked pale and strange. But Luke went straight up to him, no longer afraid. Gobby was nothing compared to what he had to contend with now.

'There's something I have to do and I need your help. I don't want to do it alone. Will you come with me?'

'It's the piccolo, isn't it?' Gobby said.

Luke said nothing, just nodded – and together they set off for Shadow Lane.

Chapter Eleven Back to the Shop

Along the dusty high street the two boys made their way, hurrying as fast as they could through the crowds of shoppers. Neither spoke, for what was there to say? Luke was obsessed, fixated with the idea of returning the piccolo to the old shop before some tragic accident occurred, but a tiny part of his mind wondered why he was bringing Gobby, of all people, with him. Why had he brought his worst enemy, the person who, until now, he had feared more than anyone? But deep down he knew. It was because of the Shadow. To Luke, the Shadow was much, much worse than anything on the planet. He couldn't face it alone.

And of all people, he knew Gobby might be

the only one who could help him now. He was the only person who had connected Luke, the piccolo, the Shadow and all the strange things that had happened at school. Perhaps being the bully he was, he was better able to understand the nature of the Shadow than even Luke. Luke was sure Gobby had seen it anyway, though the other kids hadn't.

As for Gobby, he had lived in a strange, nightmare state since the car had headed for him, intent on running him down. Gobby *had* seen the Shadow in all its horror. And he had been shocked out of his cruel attitude to life and other people. He had looked intimidation and death in the face and was afraid at last.

And Gobby was clever too. He knew something had to be done about the piccolo, and he worried that wimpy Luke couldn't handle it alone. Besides, to his surprise, Luke had asked for help. What else could he do? He'd go along to find out what was going on, what needed doing. He could worry about dealing with Luke later, couldn't he?

Luke spoke at last. 'Here it is. We go down there.'

They paused, looking down the sloping cobbled street. Shadow Lane was dark and silent.

'So what's this all about?' Gobby asked.

'We're taking the piccolo back to where it belongs.' Luke pointed down the lane. 'The music shop where Gran bought it for me is down there. It's a really odd place. I think they might know something about the piccolo and…the Shadow from inside it.'

At these words Luke stopped and both boys looked straight at each other, standing on the corner where the bright day turned into dark shade. Gobby's silence told Luke what he needed to know.

'Only you and me. We're the only two who have seen it. You must be pretty brave to have come with me,' Luke added.

'You hope!' Gobby grinned for a minute, with his old confidence. But then he seemed to remember who he was talking to. 'Come on.

Let's get it over with. I knew that stupid tin whistle was trouble!' he said roughly and ran on ahead quickly and silently. Over the cobbles, under the overhanging upper storeys of the medieval houses, past the dim, grimy shops full of antiques, curiosities, books, crystals and strange carved stones.

Luke followed. He felt very afraid of what was about to happen but very sad at the same time, at the thought of handing over his beloved instrument which he'd played better than anything else before. Now he'd be boring, ordinary, lonely Luke again back at school tomorrow. If there was a tomorrow... He pushed the thought from his mind. 'Look,' he suddenly whispered (Shadow Lane was a place where you whispered), clutching Gobby's arm.

'What?'

'The black cat!'

'So? What about it?'

'It was here before, when I first played the piccolo, and again later. I didn't notice it, but

Gran did. I think it knows about the piccolo. Gran said it danced to it, but I didn't believe her then…'

Gobby looked at him as if he was completely bonkers. But the black cat wrapped itself around their legs, leading them softly and sinuously to the shabby door of the old music shop.

'Come on,' Gobby muttered, 'let's go in.'

If only I could turn back time, thought Luke. If only none of this had happened… But Luke suddenly realised that if it hadn't happened, if he'd never found and played the piccolo, he would never have seen the admiration and amazement in his classmates' eyes when he played it. He had basked in that for a moment, at least. And if none of this had happened, he wouldn't be on the music-shop doorstep with Gobby beside him, not quite a friend, but an ally at least. The idea of that would have terrified him only a few days ago.

The black cat purred, rubbing against the

door and their legs, miaowing. Luke gripped the piccolo case in one hand and pushed the blistered and flaking door with the other.

But the door would not budge. He could not push it open. The shop was closed. Luke rang the bell. Nothing happened. He rang again. Nothing. Gobby pushed the door hard. It would not give. Luke peered through the window trying to see the old man and Leo, the young man with the floppy hair. But all he could see was a throng of instruments and the white grand piano still standing like a queen in the midst of them.

Chapter Twelve The Rose Garden

The black cat stopped pushing against the
door, looked at Luke, miaowed, then ran
further down the lane. Luke and Gobby
looked at each other, then they followed. The
cat stopped at a pointed doorway between two
of the oldest looking shops on the lane, both
empty and boarded up. The ancient bricks
round the doorway arch were covered with
carved initials and old dates. Enormous studs
held the shabby door together. Luke pushed it.
This one opened and Luke and Gobby entered
a narrow, gloomy alleyway with damp, red
bricks covered with moss and lichen. It smelt
of green wetness, for here and there fell drips
of water. They had to bend as they ran along,

so low was the alley, a dark tunnel almost, though they could see light at the end of it. They followed the cat until they emerged into autumn sunlight. There, blooming in the sun, were the gardens that lay behind the shops.

The two boys ran after the cat along a paved path, past several gardens, until they reached the one that Luke's gran had seen from the window of the square room in the music shop. Here, the cat leapt onto the grassy bank and began to wash itself, ignoring them completely. In front of Luke and Gobby was the back of the music shop, with its square window above and a dusty glass-panelled door below, leading into the shop.

The garden was full of tall reeds, grasses and flowers, with roses spreading wildly over everything. There was a high brick wall on one side and a view of the river, the quay and world beyond on the other. On the little green bank the cat was purring like an engine.

Luke approached the glass-panelled door and rapped on it. 'Is anybody there?' he called.

He wanted to see the old man and Leo desperately. He didn't want to take the piccolo back home. He had to leave it here. He was sure they would know what to do and would help him, though he didn't really know how or why.

No one answered Luke. Even the cat was silent, though its ears were pricked and alert now.

'Let's try the door,' said Gobby.

They pushed it hard, but it didn't move an inch. Gobby gave it a truly powerful shove, but it was shut tight. Together they peered through the grimy glass panels. Dimly they could just make out the many musical instruments in the shop, but there was no movement at all. The whole of Shadow Lane and its world appeared to be waiting.

'It's the spookiest place I've ever been,' Gobby muttered. Then, 'Call them again, Luke,' he whispered, to break the spell of silence.

'Sir! Leo!' Luke called. Still no one answered. 'Please come.' He waited. 'I need you. Please! Help me!'

Silence.

Luke felt suddenly shattered. What was he to do? He'd set his heart on returning the piccolo to the old man, on him knowing what to do, and now this – nothing.

The little cat waved its paw after a passing butterfly, the only sign of movement. It was all so beautiful in the garden and yet…and yet somehow…strange and oppressive.

'Play the piccolo,' Gobby said. 'Maybe that'll fetch them.'

'But the Shadow might come if I play.' Luke shuddered.

'Does it always come for the piccolo playing?' Gobby asked.

'No, at least it didn't at first. I don't know any more,' Luke replied softly, almost afraid to speak of it. What if it could hear him and came anyway? Was it the Shadow he could feel in this strange garden, hovering and preying on the edge of his consciousness. 'I think it came whenever I played when I was angry and scared. When I thought about…about what you and Cal and Clobber did to me and my flute, and how pathetic I was because I didn't stop you, not even when it was the flute my dad gave to me. But then it got so I couldn't stop it, it had nothing to do with me any—'

'But you're not scared of me now, are you, Luke?' Gobby interrupted suddenly.

'No, I suppose I'm not,' Luke said slowly, surprised.

'Then you can play and the old man and this Leo will hear it and come. They're probably here, somewhere. At the top of the house above the shop, maybe. It's so tall they can't hear us.'

'OK,' said Luke, uncertain. He called up to the window once more, to be sure. Then he got the piccolo out of its case and blew it as gently as the cat nearby patted and played with the butterfly it had captured. Gentle? Or cruel?

The notes were sweet like honey, like the scent of the roses in the garden. Luke felt his trembling subside.

Gobby looked up and grinned suddenly. 'It's going to be all right. The top window's opening. Your friends are up there. They've heard us. They'll come down, you'll see.'

But before Luke could follow his gaze, Gobby's grin dropped from his face. He screamed, 'Luke! I can't move my feet! The roses are growing all over me! Stop playing! *Stop playing*, Luke! The thorns are killing me!'

Chapter Thirteen Shadow Madness

But Luke could not stop. The piccolo was in control now and violent, discordant music poured out of it, a torrent of notes in a storm of sound.

Fat, grey clouds raced over the sun, blackening the bright sky. A fierce, cold wind sprang up, bending the trees, blowing leaves and petals helter-skelter. The world turned dark and doom-laden. Gobby screamed as he tried to free himself from the rose spikes growing and spreading over and around him, but they only dug into him more sharply, holding him so he could hardly move.

In the middle of all this, the piccolo still played its fearsome music, for much as he tried to stop, Luke couldn't. He had to play. He and the piccolo were as one.

And now the Shadow came.

Taller and even more misshapen than ever, it seemed to sway, controlling the clouds, the wind, the thorns, the roses, Gobby and Luke. They were all captives in its power. The piccolo played its demonic melody, on and on.

The Shadow's face was even clearer than before. The distorted, disturbing shape had huge pits for eyes and a gaping black hole for a mouth. Its elongated arms seemed always to be reaching out, grasping for something. It stretched those arms towards Luke and the piccolo now, to embrace and draw them in. And it spoke for the first time.

Its voice sounded like the worst notes of the piccolo's deadly tune.

'Give me the piccolo. It is mine.'

'No!' shouted Gobby, scratched and bleeding, but still full of courage. 'Luke, don't let it have it! It'll play it for ever – then it will have complete control.' It had come to Gobby in a flash. From what Luke had told him, it seemed that the Shadow still needed the piccolo and its angry playing in order to materialise properly. Surely if it had the piccolo for itself there would be no stopping it.

The Shadow swung towards Gobby, sizzling like a black electric storm.

'Luke, stop playing that thing and run!' Gobby managed to shout.

'No, give me the piccolo.' The Shadow swung back towards Luke. 'It's mine! It was always mine. But it was taken from me, with all my hate inside it.' Then it laughed gloatingly. 'You cannot move, Luke. Your pent-up hatred and fear have made you my slave. You will have to give the piccolo to me.'

Gobby was pulling steadily, carefully, painfully at the rose thorns, slowly freeing himself. 'Help! Cat! Run and fetch help. Go!' he yelled desperately.

Unbelievably, the cat leapt from the bank and ran toward the shop door like a black streak of speed. Luke, chained to the piccolo, played on, exhausted and sweating, drowning in despair. He couldn't break the spell and the Shadow was moving ever closer.

'Give me it now, or you will die. I can devour you as well as the piccolo. I can swallow you up, until you are all *me* and there is no *you* left here in this world!'

The words bored into Luke's brain, like the piccolo's screeching notes. His head felt as if it might explode. The Shadow began to pull on his arms. He wouldn't give in! Luke held on to the piccolo despite the pain in his head, hands and wrenched shoulders.

'I'm your friend.' Its words spiked like barbed wire. 'I don't really want to hurt you. Didn't I help you against your enemies? Give it to me, Luke. I will take revenge on everyone who has ever hurt you or me. Give the piccolo to me. Back where it belongs.'

Luke tightened his faltering grip on the piccolo again. What the Shadow would do with it was wrong, it mustn't have it. Luke prayed in his head, somebody please save us.

His eyes closed. The Shadow was all around him now, towering over him. He was alone and lost for ever. He tried to send out words once more...

Sir! Leo! Save me! Save us!

Still playing, he tried to push the Shadow away. But it was too strong for him to resist.

Save us, please!

The piccolo was being wrenched from his grasp. He couldn't resist any more. He'd tried. But he hadn't been good enough.

Chapter Fourteen Gran

Back at Luke's house, Gran was preparing the evening meal. She hummed as she worked, partly because she enjoyed cooking so much and partly because she felt nervous and was trying not to. Something was bothering her, making her uneasy. She just couldn't quite put her finger on it.

The phone rang.

'Mr Mezzetti? Yes, it's Luke's grandmother here. What is it?'

'Is Luke with you?'

'No. I'm just getting his tea ready, but he's not here. Isn't he at orchestra practice this evening?'

'No. And I thought it was strange – he never

misses it normally. His friend Zoe said he had been a little distracted all day. She seemed worried about him. He knows he's got this big solo part that I particularly wanted to run through with him this evening...'

'Well, he isn't here. I wonder if he can have forgotten. Perhaps he's gone to a friend's house or something.' Luke's gran said this in a perfectly normal tone, but already she had one arm in her coat and was looking for her house keys.

'I'm sure that's it. I just wanted to check – things have been a bit strange at school these last few days.'

'Strange? What do you mean?' Gran stopped her hurrying to listen.

Mr Mezzetti told her about Cal's mysterious boils and the car that had nearly run over a pupil in the playground, then disappeared.

'Well, I'm sure Luke's OK. I think I know where he will be. And I really must go now, Mr Mezzetti,' Gran said quickly as he finished speaking. She was even more worried now.

She turned off the oven, wrote a quick note

for Luke's mother and was out of the house in a flash. Heading for Shadow Lane. It seemed now that she had known it would all finish there, ever since she had first set eyes on that piccolo.

Chapter Fifteen
Shadow Battle

It was Gobby who had wrenched the piccolo from Luke. Somehow he had torn himself away from the roses' spiteful spikes to do it. And holding the piccolo, which was silent now, he was already hobbling for the shop's back door with the black cat running beside him, seeming to urge him on.

The door was open. There stood the old man and Leo. Luke ran towards them too. 'Save us!' he cried, at last able to speak.

The Shadow was huge now, seeming to loom as high as the vast grey clouds in the sky. 'Give me the piccolo!' it screamed. 'I made it and it's all mine!'

But Gobby had pushed the piccolo towards

the old man, who now clutched it to his chest. Luke crowded in behind Gobby and the cat. The Shadow lunged at the old man, grabbing at the piccolo, but it missed as they fell back in a muddled, terrified heap – into the shop's passageway, slamming the door behind them so fiercely that its dingy panes of glass rattled. Breathing hard, they could see the Shadow raging and storming outside, its contorted limbs beyond control.

'That's won us a minute or two,' panted Gobby.

The old shop seemed to shudder. A howling wind blew against it, rocking it to its foundations. Yet the building managed to stand firm against the tempest.

'It'll find it hard to cross the threshold,' said the old man.

'What does that mean?' asked Luke. 'We're safe, are we?'

'We can't really be safe with it raging outside, still on the loose. We have to stop it.'

Luke was relieved that he had chosen the

right place to bring the piccolo, but he had so many questions. Did they know what the Shadow was, how it was linked with his piccolo? If so, why had they let him take it away in the first place? But before Luke could begin, the old man seemed to sense his thoughts.

'All in good time, boy,' he whispered. 'Now we have to concentrate on capturing it.'

Behind them, the terrifying racket of the Shadow and the storm began slowly to die away and silence fell.

'What's happening?' Luke asked.

'Perhaps it's given up,' Gobby suggested.

'No, perhaps—' the old man began.

'Listen,' Leo interrupted. 'Listen!'

From the front of the shop, came a cry, 'Luke! Help me!'

'Gran! It's my gran!'

'Come on!' Gobby shouted.

They stumbled headlong through the shop's dusty interior, watched by the many musical instruments. The old man still clutched the piccolo protectively.

'Gran, I'm coming!' Luke shouted.

'It's gone round to the front and captured her,' cried Leo.

'Open the door and let her in! Before it hurts her,' Luke begged.

'Think carefully about what you are saying,' said Leo. 'The Shadow will come in as well if we do that. We may not be able to stop it.'

'Let her in. Let her in! Open the door.'

'What else can we do?' said Gobby – and he unlocked the door.

It flew open. The Shadow stood at the top of the shop's three wooden steps. Gran was enveloped in its dark arms.

'Luke, I came,' she said weakly, before fainting away.

The Shadow held her out towards them, its pitted eyes glaring blackly.

'Give me the piccolo in exchange for her. It is mine! It was always mine, but it was stolen from me.' Its voice was rasping and hollow, a crude copy of a voice.

'You cannot have it.' The old man's voice was weary, his age apparent for the first time since Luke had met him. 'You created it for good – but now you only want it for evil. If you could only forgive the past, you could be at peace. We could all be at peace.'

'Why should I forgive? What has anyone ever done for me? All I loved was taken away. But I shall have my revenge. I shall have the power to kill music for ever and destroy you all. I can enjoy it no longer – its enjoyment was taken from me, and I shall take it away from everyone else. I shall break music's heart for ever as mine has been broken.'

The hideous screeching voice rang out louder and louder, higher and higher.

'GIVE ME THE PICCOLO! Then you can have her!' The Shadow stepped threateningly into the shop, carrying Luke's gran. The door slammed shut behind it. They were all trapped.

But then the little cat leapt onto the old man's shoulder just as he lifted his arms, held the piccolo to his mouth – and blew.

There came a faint sound, a breath of noise, a note of music far, far away, very clear and clean – the high note of the piccolo, the highest in music, calling from the mountain tops, the rivers and streams, the stars in the sky. Then… came the trill of a flute, the clear round call of a clarinet, the sound of an oboe, a bassoon, the rich, warm notes of the saxophone, the sophisticated sound of a trombone, and the rallying calls of trumpets, cornets, tubas.

The Shadow's arms were no longer reaching for the old man and the piccolo. Its cavernous mouth was gaping, its arms were wrapped protectively about its head. 'Noooooo!' it screeched.

Now the percussion instruments joined in: drums, the clash of cymbals, the great big timpano drum, then the strings' melody, sweetest of all, singing into the air, violins weaving their magic along with the viola, the cello and the double bass, a harp's ripple, the zazz of electric guitars, till it seemed to Luke that all the musical instruments that had ever existed were playing, the shop was so full of melodic sound. Then...wonder of wonders...the great white piano joined in the enormous symphony of sound, lifting, raising it out of the shop, into the garden, up to the sky, where the storm clouds were streaming away beyond the horizon, leaving the bright sun shining. Every instrument in the shop was playing a song of freedom, happiness and joy, a welcoming concerto of thanks and praise for all the world's delights. And for music.

The old man took the piccolo from his mouth, stepped forward to Luke and held it out.

'Play,' he said.

Luke hesitated. What terrible things would happen if he did?

'Remember your love for music, remember what it meant to you and your father.'

Luke gasped. How did the old man know about his dad?

'Remember your love for the piccolo when you first played it,' the old man went on. 'Your playing was beautiful in the practice room that day. And that was all your doing, Luke. That was your playing, not the piccolo's. You're a talented musician.'

Suddenly Luke felt a joy that he had not felt for so long, and the wonderful music took over inside his head. He glanced once again at the Shadow, doubled up as if in pain. Then Luke gave in to his longing to join in with the other instruments, he took the piccolo and started to play.

In his thoughts, as he played, he was saying, I love you, piccolo.

At Luke's first haunting note, the Shadow gasped and writhed on the floor. Luke played on, his playing swelling into the sounds of the instruments around him. The Shadow thrashed and heaved until suddenly, its mouth open in a silent scream, it gave a huge sigh and started to wilt and diminish. Mist and shadows poured from its gaping mouth, twisting and turning wisps that took on the shape of winged insects. They wafted around the room and then slowly, slowly disappeared.

Luke's grandmother, awake again now, crawled away from the Shadow and Leo helped her to her feet. The old man and Leo supported her between them. The Shadow did nothing to stop them. It lay on the floor, howling and shrieking despairingly, noises coming from the depths of Hell. For a moment, its face came into focus and it looked almost human. Luke stared, shocked. He knew that face somehow. But as the Shadow grew smaller and smaller the face faded and the anguished cries grew fainter and fainter, until there was just a pile of fine dust left on the floor where the terrible Shadow figure had once been.

The black cat hissed and made a move towards the remains. Gobby grabbed it.

The music stopped. Luke lowered the piccolo from his mouth.

All was quiet.

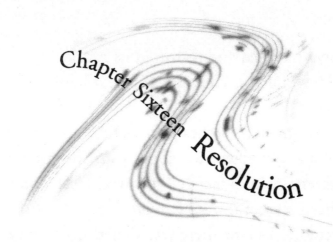

Chapter Sixteen

Resolution

It was Leo who carried Gran up to the very top of the house, above the shop. This was where he lived with the old man – his grandfather. Everyone settled into the comfort of sofas and armchairs and warm drinks. Gobby's scratches were bathed and Gran was given brandy. She soon revived.

'Tough lady!' Gobby grinned.

But to her all that mattered was Luke was safe. Although he was pale, with dark shadows under his eyes, her grandson was smiling. He seemed happier to her than he had in such a long time. He still held the precious piccolo to him but the old man had reassured them all that it was harmless now. The Shadow no longer haunted and distorted its music.

'How did you know I was here, Gran?' Luke asked.

'You missed orchestra practice and your friend Zoe was worried about you. She got Mr Mezzetti to call me. As you weren't at home either I started thinking, worrying…about the piccolo… I knew there was something strange about it from the moment I saw it.'

Zoe was worried about him! Luke felt a shiver of happiness. Perhaps he had one friend in school, after all.

'But what was it all about?' Gran went on.

'Flutes and piccolos go right back, you know,' the old man said slowly. 'Greece, Egypt, Japan, India, China, all had them, though they weren't exactly the same instruments as we play today.'

Gobby fidgeted. He wasn't used to sitting still while someone else talked, but he was trying his best.

The old man smiled at him and carried on. 'Eventually, in the 1800s, a man named

Theobald decided to improve the flute design. It's really his flute, and the piccolo based on it, that's mostly played today. Theobald was one of a large family. Boehm, the name was.'

Gran stirred a little in her chair, but said nothing.

'Amongst all the Boehm sisters, brothers and cousins was one called Walter. He didn't quite fit in and they laughed at him a lot. He was very tall and thin and lanky, always tripping over his own feet. This made him shy, so he hid away in the workshop making and playing instruments, wonderful ones. He didn't think he'd ever find someone to love him and music was his life.

'Then he met a girl called Maria. And soon he fell in love. What else do you do when you think you're the most pathetic and worst looking idiot on the face of the earth and suddenly there's this little thing with dark eyes and black curls laughing with you, not at you, and making you feel wonderful? He went crazy with happiness. He loved her madly – and he gave her the best and prettiest present he could think of, perfect for his pretty and petite sweetheart. A piccolo!

'All his instrument-making expertise and, more importantly, enormous love went into this piccolo. The one Luke is holding right now.'

From the moment the old man had started his story, Luke had known that the piccolo he was holding would be the one. He glanced down at the piccolo in his lap, then looked back at the old man as he continued.

'Quite soon they were married. He didn't notice that she hardly ever played his piccolo. He loved her so much that he saw only her. Besides, she was soon busy with their baby boy.

'But his wife loved to dance. Walter was too shy to join in, he worried that he would be laughed at. Besides, he was always playing for the dancers. Then at one party, as Walter's wife sat sadly at the edge of the room, with no partner to dance with, a very handsome young lieutenant asked her to partner him. He was a superb dancer.

'Three months later she left Walter and her little boy and ran away with the lieutenant.

'Walter went after them, taking the piccolo with him. He found out where they were lodging and stormed in, full of murderous rage. He took the piccolo to make Maria see how much he loved her, how he had tried to do so much for her in his own way, even if he couldn't be the man she wanted. But the lieutenant was the best soldier in his regiment and he was a bully. He laughed at Walter and told him he could keep his piccolo – it was his obsession with music that had lost him Maria. Then he drew his sword.

Walter couldn't fight back with a piccolo – and he was stabbed. Then the lieutenant fled with Walter's wife *and* the piccolo.

The landlord found Walter dying. In his final moments Walter cursed the piccolo, and music itself, for losing him his love and ruining his life. As he died he commanded the piccolo to seek out someone filled with anger and hate to carry out his final wishes – to punish all cruel people.'

The old man paused. Gobby raised his eyes from where he had been staring at the floor. 'The piccolo found Luke because of us bullying him, didn't it?'

'There's more to it than that, Gobby,' the old man said gently. 'Walter's little son, Joachim, was looked after by the Boehm family and for a short while all was quiet.'

He paused. He looked very tired – this was a strain for him. But he knew that the task he'd inherited was nearly finished. He took a sip of water from the glass that Leo held out to him.

'Walter's family tried to find the lieutenant to avenge Walter's death, but he'd disappeared, along with Maria and the piccolo. Then one day they tracked him down. He was living in a little, shabby, rented house in the countryside. Apparently, the lieutenant had left the army and he and Maria were quite poor, for they had little luck in anything. And when Walter's brother reached the house, late one night, he found the lieutenant in an armchair, holding the piccolo to his lips. He was quite dead.

'There was no reason for his death, the doctors said, he seemed perfectly healthy. Maria was beside her self with grief though. "The piccolo! The piccolo!" she kept crying. Not long afterwards she also died.

'The piccolo was brought back to Joachim – Walter and Maria's son – now its owner. But he hated music and, because he knew of his father's curse, he shoved the piccolo to the back of a cupboard and tried to forget all about it. However, when Joachim set off for England, to study there, the piccolo was amongst the bits and pieces he took with him. Soon Joachim fell ill. He dropped out of his studies and decided to sell the piccolo to survive. He lived on the money for a while. When that ran out he went begging on the streets, became iller and iller. He almost died.

But after a while Joachim found a friend. He helped him and set him up in a job. Joachim married his friend's sister, he learnt to be happy and they had three children and several grandchildren. Oh, and he changed his name to Bowen.'

Gran sat up. 'But that's my name!'

'And mine,' cried Luke. 'But my piccolo? Where was it?'

'The piccolo disappeared for a long time, Joachim searched for it but couldn't track it down. Once he was better and happy, he began to worry about the curse and there were rumours of it and the sorrow it caused. He opened a music shop for second-hand instruments, in the hopes that one day...but it never happened.

Joachim became obsessed with the damage he might have caused by allowing the piccolo to leave his side. He became sick once more. Eventually his wife persuaded him to sell the shop and move away. My grandfather heard of their predicament and he bought the shop, with the piccolo in it. But the one thing that Joachim insisted on was this: he told my grandfather the story and said that he must pass it on to every generation that inherited the shop. So Grandfather told my father, he told me in turn, and I told Leo, who works with me here in the shop now. Joachim was convinced that one day someone would come along whose true love of music and the piccolo would overcome the curse and the haunting upon it.

'And one day it happened – a girl came into the shop. She was thin, sad, beautiful and in a bad way. She carried an old, shabby bag and inside it was a black and silver case and inside that – well, you can guess.

'She told me to take the piccolo. She didn't want money for it. She just wanted rid of it. She said it had brought her only hatred and had destroyed her love of music.

'I took it from her and insisted on giving her some money. And Leo, he fell in love with her. She is ill but he visits her in hospital. We hope she will recover.

The floppy hair fell over Leo's face, hiding his feelings. Gobby nearly said something, but didn't. I'm becoming considerate, he thought, pleased.

'Then, a week ago a boy came in with his grandmother to buy a flute and I could see he was the one at last. The one who would release the piccolo's shadowy powers, but enable them to be broken also. The rest you know.'

'How could you tell?' Luke asked.

'You looked just like the photograph of Joachim's father that I have – the one Joachim gave to my family when they bought the business. And the piccolo picked you. It was obvious.'

'Like the face on the dying Shadow,' Luke said wonderingly.

'I had to let you take it, in the hope that the curse would be broken for ever. Little Black here,' he picked up the little black cat, 'has been keeping an eye on you for me.'

'But why did the piccolo pick *Luke*? Like you said, he freed the Shadow, but he stopped it eventually too,' said Gobby.

'I think I know,' Luke said quietly.

'Go on, Luke,' said the old man.

'The Shadow of Walter in the piccolo thought

I was like it, that I hated like it did, that because I was bullied too, like Walter, I would allow it to carry out its revenge, whatever it took. But Walter's mistake was to blame music for losing him his wife. He lost her without music's help, because he didn't believe in and stand up for himself. As soon as I saw that what was happening wasn't right, I started to stand up for myself. The piccolo, the Shadow, didn't like that. It tried to bully me into doing what it wanted anyway. I think, because I was able to rise above it, face my fears and play the piccolo for pure joy again, I grew stronger than the bitter, twisted Shadow.

'But can I keep the piccolo?' Luke asked.

'Of course. It belongs in your family after all.'

Luke, Gran and Gobby walked dazedly down the stairs to the shop. Leo and his grandfather came down with them. The little pile of dust still lay on the shop floor.

'We ought to scatter the ashes and lay him to rest at last,' said Gran.

She swept the ashes into a little dish, then they went out into the garden, where the roses bloomed sweetly, and scattered the poor, sad, doomed ashes on the earth.

Luke couldn't forget that, despite everything, the Shadow had shown him so much about himself and how strong he could be. Perhaps one day soon he would find a way to make his mum see this too.

And the little cat danced along with them, as the stars came out and shone in the night sky.

One last thing.

A few days later, three boys came to orchestra practice.

'We want to join, Sir,' announced Gobby. 'I reckon I could get quite good at playing an instrument. Stop fidgeting, Clobber. And I've told them they want to learn to play and they've agreed. OK?' He stuck his thumb in Cal and Clobber's direction.

'OK.' Mr Mezzetti grinned.

And that's how at the end-of-term concert Gobby was blowing a trumpet, Cal was on a recorder and Clobber joined Zoe on the drums (he showed talent, according to Mr Mezzetti). After the solos and songs, Luke played the piccolo and the flute in a performance of *Peter and the Wolf*.

Among the admiring audience sat Luke's grandmother and mother, the old man (beard freshly trimmed) and Leo (hair even floppier), taking great care of a very thin, very lovely girl with long golden hair, on the seat beside him. Next to them, Zoe's parents had seats. They all applauded loudly at the end of the show. No shadows anywhere.

But even then Gobby was planning a breakaway group playing heavy metal.

ORCHARD RED APPLES

All priced at £4.99

Orchard Red Apples are available from all good bookshops,
or can be ordered direct from the publisher: Orchard Books,
PO BOX 29, Douglas IM99 1BQ
Credit card orders please telephone 01624 836000
or fax 01624 837033or visit our Internet site: www.wattspub.co.uk
or e-mail: bookshop@enterprise.net for details.

To order please quote title, author and ISBN
and your full name and address.
Cheques and postal orders should be made payable to 'Bookpost plc.'
Postage and packing is FREE within the UK
(overseas customers should add £1.00 per book).
Prices and availability are subject to change.